DEC 2015

Companion and Therapy Animals

Kelli Hicks

Rourke
Educational Media

rourkeeducationalmedia.com

Scan for Related Titles
and Teacher Resources

Before Reading:

Building Academic Vocabulary and Background Knowledge

Before reading a book, it is important to tap into what your child or students already know about the topic. This will help them develop their vocabulary, increase their reading comprehension, and make connections across the curriculum.

1. *Look at the cover of the book. What will this book be about?*
2. *What do you already know about the topic?*
3. *Let's study the Table of Contents. What will you learn about in the book's chapters?*
4. *What would you like to learn about this topic? Do you think you might learn about it from this book? Why or why not?*
5. *Use a reading journal to write about your knowledge of this topic. Record what you already know about the topic and what you hope to learn about the topic.*
6. *Read the book.*
7. *In your reading journal, record what you learned about the topic and your response to the book.*
8. *After reading the book complete the activities below.*

Content Area Vocabulary
Read the list. What do these words mean?

anxious
comfort
companion
extensive
handler
impairments
navigate
protective
seizure
service animals
temperament
verbal

After Reading:

Comprehension and Extension Activity

After reading the book, work on the following questions with your child or students in order to check their level of reading comprehension and content mastery.

1. *Why do service animals wear a vest?* (Asking questions)
2. *Where do companion and service dogs usually come from?* (Summarize)
3. *Do you have a pet? How does your pet make you feel? Share with us.* (Text to self connection)
4. *Why is the temperament of an animal a factor when selecting companion or service animals?* (Inferring)
5. *How can a service animal help during a handler's seizure?* (Summarize)

Extension Activity

Are there therapy animal organizations near you? Look up your state at www.therapydoginfo.net/organizations.html and see what organizations are offered. What services are provided? What types of animals offer these services? What are some ways you can help? Create awareness by creating a poster educating others about therapy animals and ways they can help.

Table of Contents

Chapter 1
What is a Companion?

A beautiful reddish-orange dog wags his tail in a friendly manner. The golden retriever is obviously well cared for, neatly groomed, and the dog looks content. The vest the dog is wearing, however, shows that he is not your usual pet. This retriever is a working animal. A special **companion** or **service animal** provides assistance to its **handler** who is in a wheelchair and sometimes needs help to take care of day to day activities. Some people use animals as companions to help make their lives better.

Medical professionals have long recognized that animals can assist people with physical disabilities, including people who are blind or deaf.

There are many different kinds of working animals. Most often, dogs are the helpers. But cats, horses, dolphins, birds, rabbits, lizards, and even elephants can work as companion or therapy animals.

FURRY FACT

Animals can make a big difference to children with autism or Asperger's. Therapy with horses has many benefits including helping children relax, developing motor skills, and stimulating communication.

Service dogs are also trained to provide assistance to children with autism or Asperger's. They can help calm a child or protect a child who wanders.

Chapter 2
Becoming a Companion

How does an animal become a companion? Most often, volunteers rescue animals from shelters or save them from a home where they experienced neglect or abuse. Sometimes the animals are purchased from select breeders. Volunteers or foster families then begin specialized training to prepare the animals to be companions. Some animals are better suited to the job of a companion than others. Most companion dogs are Labrador or golden retrievers, although other dogs can be trained as well.

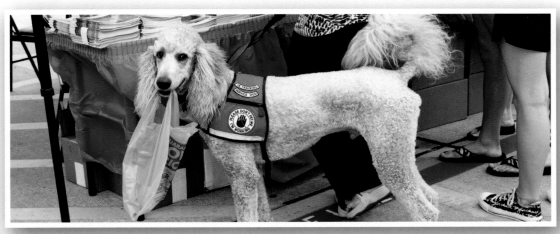

It can take up to 6 months of training for a dog to be certified as a companion animal. And an additional training session with the companion the animal is matched with to see if they are compatible.

This service dog is wearing a special harness but it is important to realize that not all service animals wear special harnesses or vests.

Important factors need to be considered when selecting an animal to serve as a companion. What is the **temperament** of the animal and how well does it respond to and interact with people? The size of the animal is important, too. Small animals might have difficulty picking up objects or retrieving items for their handlers. Large dogs will not fit under a table in public and will not fit on an airplane or on a bus. Companion animals should need very little grooming and should not be overly **protective**. Their job is to provide care and assistance, not to be a guard animal.

Service dogs are mild-mannered dogs. When you see them out, they are calm. They don't bark or chase after other dogs.

A TRIBUTE TO YUKON

Everybody needs to feel loved, to have someone they can depend on and trust. For many elementary school students, Yukon was that friend. Every day that Yukon reported to work, he understood his kids and treated them with love and would listen to them read. By the way, Yukon is a dog. He is a highly trained certified therapy dog who worked wonders with low achieving readers.

Kerry, Yukon's handler, introduced her community to CARE, a Canine Assisted Reading Program. Yukon helped reluctant and shy students to communicate, helped students with challenges to make good choices, and greeted everyone with love. He showed everyone how to deal with adversity when he was diagnosed with cancer, but still came to work every day to spend his time with the kids. He eventually lost his battle, but his memory lives on in the hearts of the hundreds of students he cared for.

Chapter 3
Training for the Job

Some dogs receive **extensive** training to assist their handlers with daily tasks. These service animals can help their handlers in many different ways. Some dogs help people in wheelchairs reach items or open and close doors. They also know when their handler is in trouble and can bark to get someone to come help. If barking doesn't work, they can go get a person to help. Guide dogs can help handlers with vision **impairments** to **navigate** in their homes or in their community independently. Hearing dogs are trained to touch their handlers with a paw to notify them of important sounds.

FURRY FACT

Service animals have become a very important part of life for many veterans. Many suffered injuries that caused them to need to use a wheelchair or lost their hearing or sight. Others have post traumatic stress disorder (PTSD). PTSD service animals are trained to provide a calming effect, sense of security, and reduce anxiety for the handler.

Training to be a service animal is a challenging process. The animal has to respond to commands both at home and when out in public. It involves more than just obeying simple commands to sit and stay. Service animals must be very well behaved and be trained to perform several different tasks to help their handler. They need to respond to both **verbal** commands and hand signals. The handlers also receive training to know how to give commands appropriately and how to care for their animals.

It is important that the dog and handler understand and communicate well with each other to be a successful match.

FURRY FACT

There are many animals that are companion animals. However, currently the American Disabilities Association only defines "dogs that are individualy trained to do work or perform tasks for people with disabilities" as service animals as well as some miniature horses. Many different organizations train dogs for the different services they perform.

Chapter 4
Saving a Life

Some companion animals or service dogs can sense medical emergencies for their handlers. **Seizure** dogs can sense when a person is going to have a seizure. That way, they can be sure that help is nearby or that the handler is somewhere safe so that they don't get hurt. Other dogs, called seizure response dogs, know how to help their handler during a seizure. They might roll the person over to make sure they can breathe or they might press an alert button to call for help.

The intense training these dogs receive and the relationship they have with their handlers allows for them to sense ahead of time when a tragedy may occur.

Cats and dogs that notice drops in blood sugar have helped people with diabetes. These animals sense that the blood sugar level is off and can bring juice or medicine to a person to prevent them from going into diabetic shock. They can also provide assistance with balance or support, or alert someone else that there is a problem.

The senses and keen response of these animals in a crisis situation can be the difference between life and death for their handlers.

Some animals provide a different type of support to people. Therapy animals provide **comfort** to people. Animals don't judge and can help people to feel safe and secure. A gentle touch can reduce a patient's fear or simply make someone feel loved. Social animals are trained to help reduce stress for people who are **anxious** or scared to leave their homes. Some elderly care facilities or childrens' homes utilize therapy animals to work with their residents.

Therapy animals have been proven to be a valuable asset, especially in a clinical environment. The patient's response is immediate.

MEET SCOOBY BOO

Standing only 29.5 inches (74.9 centimeters) tall, a mini horse named Scooby Boo Bidwell is small, but has a gigantic impact on the lives of others. Cared for well in his early years, eight-year-old Boo found himself neglected and in need of medical help. With the love and care of a new family, Boo was able to provide comfort and care to others. Boo's handler Robin took him on his first outing to a nursing home and he connected with the residents immediately. He instinctively seems to know what each person he visits needs and provides them with hope, reminds them of happy times, or just simply provides unconditional love and comfort.

When Boo visits, he brings with him information about the therapeutic benefits of horses and wears clean tennis shoes indoors. Can you believe Boo is potty trained as well?

Robin Bidwell with Scooby Boo

Companion and service animals not only help people facing challenges they find hard to overcome, but also make the quality of life for these individuals happier and healthier just by giving their love and support. They are true life savers!

To some people, life without these amazing animals would be unbearable. As a true companion, they help people overcome and deal with many fears as well as disabilities.

How Can You Help?

You can collect donations for or hold a fundraiser for a local organization that trains companion or service animals.

You can learn about therapy animals in your area and find out how you can support the animal.

You can tell others what you know about companion animals and help spread the word about the impact these special animals can have on people.

You can volunteer your time to help out at a shelter.

You can write a letter to the newspaper or contribute to a blog about a companion or therapy animal that you know.

You can show respect for service animals by not taking your pet to places that say "No pets allowed. Service Animals only."

Glossary

anxious (ANGK-shuhs): worried or fearful

comfort (KUHM-fort): the feeling of being at ease, calming or reassuring

companion (kuhm-PAN-yuhn): a reliable friend, someone you spend time with

extensive (ek-STEN-siv): spreading over a wide area, including lots of things

handler (HAND-ler): a person who is in charge of a specially trained dog

impairments (im-PAIR-ments): things that hold people back from being able to live or function on their own

navigate (NAV-uh-gate): to travel, find your way

protective (pruh-TEK-tiv): guarding from attack, injury, or danger

seizure (SEE_zhur): a sudden attack of an illness, spasms that affect how someone functions

service animals (SUR-vis AN-uh-muhlz): defined as dogs and some miniature horses that are highly trained to assist a person with a disability

temperament (TEM-pur-uh-muhnt): ones nature or personality, the way one thinks or responds to other people or situations

verbal (VUR-buhl): expressed in spoken words

Index

Show What You Know

1. What qualities make a good companion animal?
2. Who can benefit from having a companion animal?
3. How extensive is the training required to be certified as a companion animal?
4. How is a therapy animal similar to a companion animal? How are they different?
5. What can kids do to help support working animals?

Websites to Visit

www.petakids.com/animal-facts/companion-animals
www.nhes.org/articles/view/316
www.pbs.org/parents/martha/helpinganimals/index.html

About the Author

Kelli Hicks is a teacher and author who lives in Tampa, Florida. She supports her local pet shelter and recently adopted a rescue puppy named Emma June. Emma is much too excitable to work as a companion, but she does keep Kelli company as she writes.

Meet The Author!
www.meetREMauthors.com

www.rourkeeducationalmedia.com

PHOTO CREDITS: Cover © Robert J. Daveant; p1 © Monkey Business Images; p4 © Boris Djuranovic; p5, pg9 © Jeroen van den Broek; p5 © IS_ImageSource, bluecrayola; p6 © tifonimages; p7 ©jonya; p8 © fstop123; p10 © c_taylor; p11 © Kerry Callahan; p12 © Micimakin; p13 © DoublePHOTO studio; p14 © Cylonphoto; p15 © Steve Shoup; p16 © Zipster969; p17 © alarich; p18 © iofoto; p19 © Robin Bidwell; p20 Public Domain; p21 © viviolsen, © Cathy Yeulet

Edited by: Luana Mitten

Cover and Interior design by: Jen Thomas

Library of Congress PCN Data

Companion and Therapy Animals (Animal Matters)
  ISBN 978-1-63430-068-1 (hard cover)
  ISBN 978-1-63430-098-8 (soft cover)
  ISBN 978-1-63430-124-4 (e-Book)
Library of Congress Control Number: 2014953374

Printed in the United States of America, North Mankato, Minnesota

Also Available as: